FLOWERS

Rosamund Kidman Cox
Barbara Cork

Designed by David Bennett
and Candice Whatmore
Cover design by Josephine Thompson
Cover illustration by Isabel Bowring

Illustrated by Wendy Bramall, Mark Burgess,
Michelle Emblem, Denise Finney, Sarah Fox-Davies,
Sheila Galbraith, Victoria Gooman, David Hurrell, Mick Loates,
Andy Martin, Dee Morgan, Cynthia Pow and Ralph Stobart

Edited by Laura Howell
Consultant editor: Mary Gibby Ph.D.
Language consultant: Betty Root

Contents

Looking at flowers

If you look closely at a flower, you will see that it is made of many different parts.

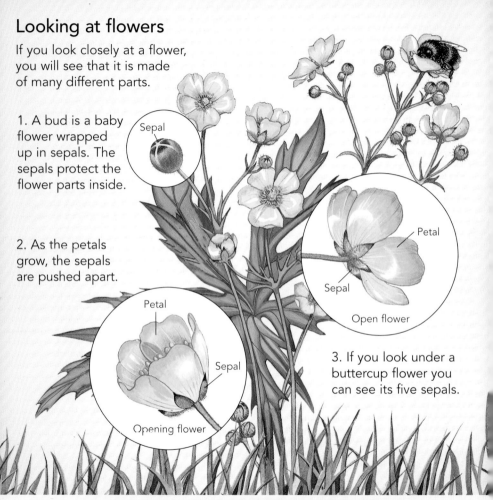

1. A bud is a baby flower wrapped up in sepals. The sepals protect the flower parts inside.

Sepal

2. As the petals grow, the sepals are pushed apart.

Petal

Sepal

Petal

Sepal

Open flower

Petal

Sepal

Opening flower

3. If you look under a buttercup flower you can see its five sepals.

Go to **www.usborne-quicklinks.com** for a link to a Web site where you can learn about plant life by solving the mystery of the Great Plant Escape.

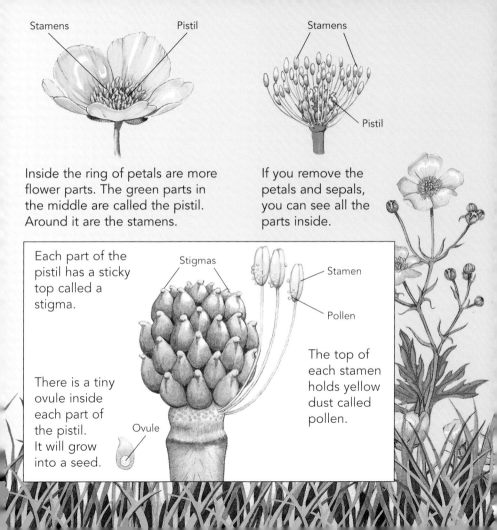

Stamens   Stamens

Pistil

Pistil

Inside the ring of petals are more flower parts. The green parts in the middle are called the pistil. Around it are the stamens.

If you remove the petals and sepals, you can see all the parts inside.

Each part of the pistil has a sticky top called a stigma.

Stigmas

Stamen

Pollen

There is a tiny ovule inside each part of the pistil. It will grow into a seed.

Ovule

The top of each stamen holds yellow dust called pollen.

Looking at flower parts

Most types of flowers have the same parts, but they may seem very different. You need to look closely at each flower to see which part is which.

Bindweed

Harebell

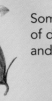

Some have petals of different shapes and sizes.

Violet

Some flowers have petals joined together.

Lily

Bottlebrush

Some have lots of stamens.

Some have bright sepals and petals.

Fuchsia

Pink

Vetch

Columbine

Go to www.usborne-quicklinks.com for a link to a Web site where you can examine many flowers, and spot how their petals and sepals are different.

Stigma

Some flowers have a pistil with only one stigma.

Daffodil

Stigmas

Some have a pistil with more than one stigma.

Crocus

Cranesbill

An aster flower is made of lots of tiny flowers.

In the middle of the aster are many tiny yellow flowers.

Each flower around the outside has one long petal.

There is a bumblebee somewhere on this page. Do you know why it visits flowers? The answer is on the next page.

Daisy

Dandelion

Dahlia

Flower visitors

Cranesbill

Flowers have many visitors. They are usually insects, such as bees. Bumblebees visit flowers to drink a sweet liquid called nectar. Sometimes the visitors eat some of the flower's pollen.

Yellow flag

A visitor to this flower needs a long tongue to reach down to the nectar.

Nectar is in here.

Many flowers have guide lines or dots that point the way to the nectar.

Pink

Most flowers are very bright and have a powerful scent so visitors can find them. Butterflies like to visit pink, red and blue flowers.

Honeysuckle

Most moths drink nectar at night. They visit flowers that have a sweet scent. These flowers are easy to find in the dark.

The flowers help the visitors by giving them food. The visitors also help the flowers. Do you know what the visitors do? The answer is on the next page.

This Australian honey possum is drinking nectar.

Gum tree flower

Nectar is at the bottom of the stamens.

Stamen

Go to www.usborne-quicklinks.com for a link to a Web site where you can find a detailed description of the tricks flowers use to attract visitors. Lots of pictures.

Why do flowers need visitors?

Visitors help plants by moving pollen from flower to flower.

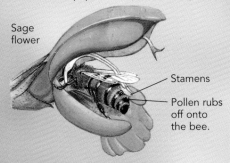

Sage flower

Stamens

Pollen rubs off onto the bee.

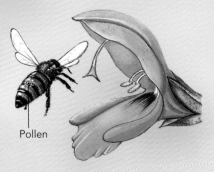

Pollen

1. As a bee collects nectar from a flower, its body gets covered with pollen.

2. It flies to another sage flower. It has pollen from the first flower on its back.

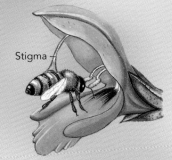

Stigma

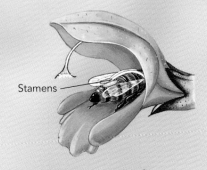

Stamens

3. As it lands, the pollen on the bee's body rubs onto the stigma of the flower.

4. The bee goes into the flower. New pollen from the stamens rubs onto its back.

Fuchsia

Hummingbird

The hummingbird on the right is drinking nectar from a fuchsia flower. It has some pollen from another fuchsia flower on its breast feathers. As the bird drinks nectar, the pollen on its feathers rubs onto the stigma of this fuchsia flower.

Watching for visitors

Find a flower that has stamens and a stigma that are easy to see. When the sun is out, sit down and wait quietly for the insects to come.

Tulip

When the insect flies away, look to see if it has left any pollen on the stigma of your flower.

If an insect comes, try to see if it has any pollen on its body.

Go to www.usborne-quicklinks.com for a link to a Web site where you can find out which flowers attract different kinds of butterflies.

How the wind helps flowers

The flowers on this page do not need visitors to move their pollen. The wind blows it from flower to flower.

Plantain flowers

False oat grass flowers

These flowers have no scent or bright petals to attract visitors.

Plantain

Instead, they have many stamens with lots of pollen. The wind blows it away.

In the spring, you may see clouds of pollen blowing off grass flowers. Most of this pollen will be wasted, but some will stick onto the stigmas of other grass flowers.

Wood-rush flowers

Rye flowers

Go to www.usborne-quicklinks.com for a link to a Web site where you can find out lots about seeds, nuts and fruits, and how they are scattered.

All trees have flowers. Many trees use the wind to move their pollen.

The walnut tree has two kinds of flowers. One kind of flower has a large pistil.

The other kind of flower is made of lots of stamens.

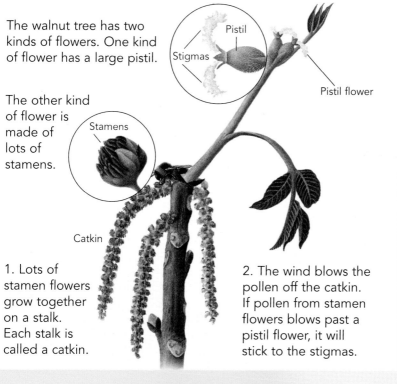

Pistil

Stigmas

Pistil flower

Stamens

Catkin

1. Lots of stamen flowers grow together on a stalk. Each stalk is called a catkin.

2. The wind blows the pollen off the catkin. If pollen from stamen flowers blows past a pistil flower, it will stick to the stigmas.

Pistil flower

Hazel tree flowers

Stamen flowers

Larch tree flowers

Stamen flowers

Pistil flowers

What happens to the pollen?

1. A bee has left pollen on this flower's stigma. The pollen came from another poppy flower.

2. Each grain of pollen grows a tube down inside the pistil. There are tiny, egg-like ovules inside the pistil.

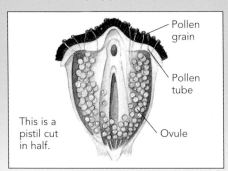

3. When a tube reaches an ovule, the inside of the pollen grain moves down the tube and joins with the ovule.

4. The ovules in the pistil have been fertilized by the pollen. The fertilized ovules will grow into poppy seeds.

Go to www.usborne-quicklinks.com for a link to a Web site where you can watch a short animated movie about pollination.

The flowers on the poppy plant can be fertilized only when an insect brings pollen from another poppy plant.

A poppy flower cannot use its own pollen to fertilize its own ovules. The pollen will not grow tubes down into the pistil.

Poppy pollen will not grow tubes in a buttercup pistil.

Buttercup flowers

More about pollen

Most flowers are like the poppy. They do not use their own pollen to fertilize themselves. Pollen must be brought from another flower of the same kind by visitors or by the wind.

A single flower of the yellow mountain saxifrage below can never fertilize itself because the stamens die before the stigmas are ripe.

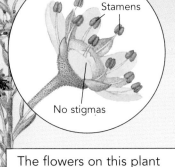

Stamens

No stigmas

Stigmas

Old stamen

The flowers on this plant are less than a week old. Only the stamens are ripe.

The flowers on this plant are more than eleven days old. The stigmas are ripe, but the stamens are dead.

Go to **www.usborne-quicklinks.com** for a link to a Web site where you can find pictures, information and video clips of pollen being carried from flowers.

The pollen of this bee orchid is moved only by male Eucera bees. But if no Eucera bees visit the orchid it will use its own pollen to fertilize itself.

Two sacs of pollen

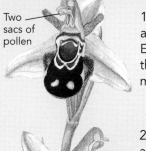

1. This bee orchid looks and smells like a female Eucera bee. This is how the orchid attracts male Eucera bees.

2. If a male bee lands on a flower, the two pollen sacs stick to his head.

Pollen

Stigma is in here.

3. Below is a different male Eucera bee. He has pollen on his head from another bee orchid.

4. As he lands on this flower, the pollen will stick onto the stigma and fertilize the flower.

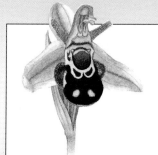

If no bees visit this bee orchid, it will fertilize itself.

The stamens bend over.

The pollen sacs touch the stigma.

This is how the bee orchid fertilizes itself.

How seeds leave the plant

1. The ovules in this poppy pistil have been fertilized. They are growing into seeds.

2. The pistil swells. It is now a fruit with seeds inside.

3. Holes open in the top. When the wind blows the fruit, the seeds fall out.

The fruit has now dried up and died.

Looking inside a seed

This is a bean seed. It has a thick skin to protect the parts inside.

If you split open a bean seed, this is what you will see inside.

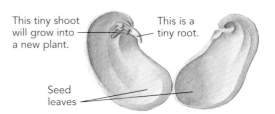

This tiny shoot will grow into a new plant.

This is a tiny root.

Seed leaves

These are two seed leaves, which are full of food. The shoot will use this food when it grows.

Go to www.usborne-quicklinks.com for a link to a Web site where you can look at different kinds of fruits and seeds, with helpful diagrams.

When the seeds in the fruits are ripe, the wind or animals may move them away from the plant.

Birds eat fruits and drop the seeds.

Maple tree fruits spin to the ground because of their special shape.

Sometimes animals bury fruits to eat later. The seeds that do not get eaten may grow into new plants.

The cranesbill fruit springs open and its seeds fly out.

The wind blows away the dandelion fruits.

Buttercup fruits may catch onto the fur of animals.

Plants make lots of seeds but only a few of them will grow into new plants. The others die or get eaten.

How a seed grows

1. Autumn
A bird drops a sunflower seed by accident.

2. Winter
The seed falls to the ground and gets covered over.

3. Spring
Rain makes the seed swell. A root grows down into the soil.

4. Spring
The shoot grows up to the light.

Seed leaves

5. Spring

Proper leaves start to grow. They will make food.

The baby plant uses the food in the seed leaves to grow.

The root takes water and minerals from the soil.

Nasturtium

Pea

Oak acorn

Sycamore

Go to www.usborne-quicklinks.com for a link to a Web site where you can learn more about sunflowers and how they grow.

6. Late spring

The sunflower plant grows a flower bud. The plant is now taller than a person.

Bud

7. Summer

The bud opens. Bees bring pollen from other sunflowers.

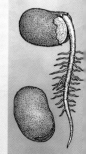

Broad bean

8. Autumn

The flowers have been fertilized.

A bird eats the seeds.

The seeds pass through the bird's body, fall to the ground, and the process begins again.

Maize

Acacia

Sweet pea

19

How insects help flowers

Flowers make most nectar and scent when their pistil or stamens are ripe, because this is when they need to attract visitors.

Bees visit these cherry flowers in the morning. This is when the flowers have most nectar.

New honeysuckle flowers open in the evening. This is when moths visit them.

Bees visit these apple flowers in the afternoon. This is when the flowers have most nectar.

The flowers make lots of scent in the evening, but only a little scent in the day.

Go to www.usborne-quicklinks.com for a link to a Web site where you can find detailed information about how and why plants attract insects.

Many plants take several weeks to open all their flowers. Bees come back to these plants day after day until all the flowers have opened.

The willowherb takes about a month to open all its flowers. The first flowers to open are at the bottom of the stem. The last flowers to open are at the top of the stem.

Willowherb (also known as fireweed)

New horse chestnut tree flowers open every day. They have lots of nectar. Yellow guide lines point the way to the nectar.

New guide lines

Old guide lines

When the nectar is finished the guide lines turn red. Bees do not visit old flowers with red guide lines.

As each flower gets older, it makes more nectar. Bees always visit older willowherb flowers first.

Keeping pollen safe

Most flowers try to keep their pollen safe and dry. Cold weather, rain and dew could damage the pollen or wash it away.

When flowers are closed, the pollen is kept safe.

Pasque flower

Crocus

When flowers are closed, rain and dew cannot get inside.

Ox-eye daisy

Daisy

These flowers come out in early spring. The flowers open only when it is warm and sunny. If the sun goes in, they close up their petals. The flowers open again when the sun comes out.

These flowers close in the evening and in bad weather. If they have to stay closed for several days, they will fertilize themselves.

Go to www.usborne-quicklinks.com for a link to a Web site where you can find amazing facts about plants and flowers.

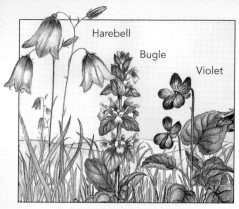

Harebell

Bugle

Violet

These flowers do not need to close their petals to keep the pollen safe. Water cannot collect inside them.

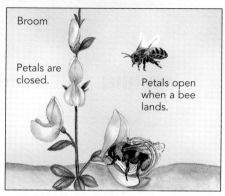

Broom

Petals are closed.

Petals open when a bee lands.

The stamens and the pistil of the broom flower are kept safe inside the petals. They spring out when a bee lands on the bottom petals.

Stamen has not split.

Pollen

Stamen has split.

Ripe stamens of apple tree flowers split open to let out the pollen. The stamens will split open only on warm days.

Catchfly flowers

Moth

New catchfly flowers open in the evening. This is when moths visit them. If the evenings are very cold, no new flowers will open.

23

Index

First published in 2002 by Usborne Publishing Ltd., Usborne House, 83-85 Saffron Hill, London EC1N 8RT, England.
www.usborne.com Copyright © 2002, 1990, 1982 Usborne Publishing Ltd.